# ATHLETES AND ARTISTS
Stories

# ATHLETES
## AND
# ARTISTS

### STORIES

## AGNES ROSSI

NEW YORK UNIVERSITY PRESS
New York *and* London

Copyright © 1987 by New York University
Manufactured in the United States of America

Library of Congress Cataloging-in-Publication Data

Rossi, Agnes, 1957–
    Athletes and artists.

    Contents: Bums on needles and pins—Athletes &
artists—Notes—[etc.]
    I. Title.
PS3568.084694A94    1987        813'.54        87-1688
ISBN 0-8147-7400-8

*Book designed by Laiying Chong.*

# CONTENTS

# BUMS ON NEEDLES AND PINS

I come up the stairs and see that the door to my apartment is wide open. Oh my God we've been robbed, I think, bracing myself for a mess. There isn't any. I look in the kitchen and bathroom for Laura. She's not either place. I check the bedroom door. It's locked.

"You can't come in here unless you hate men."

Her voice sounds like her head is under the covers.

"The front door was open," I say. "Did you know that?"

She doesn't answer.

"Laura?"

The door opens and there she is with a blue sheet wrapped around her shoulders and head, "I hate 'em," she says.

"What did he do?"

She settles herself back on the bed, which is a mess of blankets and sheets, none of them tucked in at the bottom. She lifts one leg and looks at her foot. "Charlie—no, Chuck, Chuckles the clown—has been up for three days, wired out of his

I

mind. He broke into his parents' house at six o'clock this morning and stole a bottle of gin. His father watched him climb out the laundry room window."

"We have to go to yoga," I say. Me and Laura take yoga at the Y on Monday nights. It was her idea.

"I can't go. I'm despondent."

"Come on. It'll do you good. Get a couple of complete breaths into you."


When we walk in the class has already started. There's a man in our spot, second row of mats, right-hand side. Michelle, the teacher, stares at us but goes on with the opening relaxer. "Let it go and breathe. Surrender your weight to the floor beneath you." We lie down on the front mat and start relaxing.

Michelle wears a black unitard and there is absolutely no overhang between her cheeks and the tops of her thighs. Laura calls her the bumless wonder. Michelle's rear look like my forearm, like she has two big forearms back there.

"Okay, one final breath. In and out with control. And get up. Let's work on our tadasinas."

I hate tadasina. It's just standing still but you have to tuck your buttocks in, push your abdomen towards your spine, drop your shoulders from your ears, keep your feet parallel, and open up your ribs front and back. Michelle walks around while you're doing all of this, adjusting people's bodies with her hands.

I feel like my rear end has no business in tadasina. It's too big to tuck. It needs an arched spine, which is a serious crime in yoga, for support. Michelle says Americans have the worse backs in the world, jammed lower vertebrae. I think I have an American back because I have an American rear end.

I am concentrating, really concentrating, on elongating my

spine but all of a sudden I lose my center of balance and have to open my eyes to keep from falling. Laura looks a lot better than she did when she had the sheet on her head. She's very serious about yoga, says it helps her manage stress. She's generally calmer for about a half an hour after each class, then, boom, she's back to normal.

I close my eyes because Michelle is coming toward me. She runs her hand back and forth on the base of my spine. "Let it go," she says. She means my impulse to arch. Her mouth is about three inches from my neck. If I wasn't embarrassed I'd ask her what I'm supposed to do with my rear end.


Charlie is addicted to cocaine and he's a wonderful guy. No mood swings or paranoia, at least not around us. Of course, he does disappear a couple of times a month and we get bad reports, mostly from his sister, who I don't understand. Why is she always ready to gossip about her brother? She thinks I'm Laura when I answer the phone. She'll say, "Hiiiii, it's me. Guess what?" I have to say, "Whoa. Wait a minute. This isn't Laura."

I try to remember that the whole Charlie thing is different for Laura because she's in love. She really is. But I can't help thinking that since Charlie never pretended to be anything but a fiend with a personality, Laura should have known what she was in for.

Still, Charlie is the kind of guy whose car you're glad to see parked out front when you get home from work. It's a big white Thunderbird with nicks and dents all over it, the perfect Charlie-car. The doors are huge, weigh hundreds of pounds each. You really know you're inside something when you shut one of them after yourself.

3

Charlie is sitting forward on the couch, hands clasped, elbows on his knees, telling us about when he and his sister were ten and eleven and there was a big flood that washed all of these dead bullfrogs out of a pond and onto the street. They decided to bury them so they went around with a shopping cart and collected them. They dug a hole in their backyard and had an animal funeral and all. That night a muffled bellowing noise came from the grave. It woke Charlie up. He said he knew right away what it was so he ran outside and started to dig. The frogs were alive and moaning. They hadn't been dead, they'd just been in shock or something. He had to get down on his stomach and run his hands through the mud to get them out. He turned the hose on them and they started to hop. His mother was at the window the whole time screaming, "What the hell is going on out there?"

Charlie looks great telling this story and Laura looks calm and beautiful listening. Still smiling and shaking his head, he goes in Laura's wallet to get her Visa card, which he needs to chop lines.

It's hard not to love a guy who sat up in his bed when he was ten and said, "Oh, no. The frogs."


Laura won't go to yoga because Charlie is here. I don't feel like going either, but they hardly ever get to be alone. (Me and Laura only have one bedroom so they have sex on the couch after I go to bed, then they put some clothes back on and creep into Laura's bed to sleep. All three of us snore.) Besides, yoga was sixty-two dollars for a ten-week session so it would bother me too much not to go.

4

In the Cobra position you lie on your belly and lift your shoulders off of the mat without, of course, arching your back. Again my rear end feels like it's in the way. I know I could get a better Cobra if I didn't have two big lumps of flesh messing up the line.

You're not supposed to think while you do yoga, but that's hard for beginners so we have to try not to pay attention to our thoughts. Michelle says we shouldn't be attached to them, just let them slip by us while we concentrate on our breathing.

I'm in my usual spot on the mat, second-row, far right. Nobody took Laura's spot. I guess they figured she might come in late.

"Extend from your middle finger to your second toe," Michelle says. "Pretend there's a cord running right through you."

The night we met Charlie we left Nobody's Inn with him and went for a ride in the T-Bird. We knew—well, I knew anyway—that one of us, either me or Laura, was going to be Charlie's girlfriend. We were neck and neck for awhile, then I dropped out. I have this survival thing that saves my life and keeps it boring.

Michelle's ankles are right in front of my eyes. She leans over me, puts both of her hands on the small of my back and presses hard. "No arch," she says.


Laura comes home with eyeliner on and a fashion mag under her arm so I know it's going to be a he's-out-of-my-life-for-good week. She'll eat breakfast every day and listen to radio psychologists, female ones if she can get them.

"Yoga tonight," she says. "I can't wait."

5

The part of yoga that makes me laugh is all of the talk about internal organs. Michelle will be doing a head-to-toe relaxer and when she gets to the midsection she'll say, "Release your large intestine." The Triangle pose is supposed to make you feel which of your lungs has the greater capacity for air.

I guess I've never really believed all of that stuff is inside of me, felt sure that if they sliced me at the belly button I'd look like London broil. Thinking about your liver wafting and gurgling there in the dark is like looking around your apartment and remembering that people you don't know lived there before you. They pulled doors closed and looked up at the ceilings.

Laura is still not seeing Charlie, but the eye pencil is gone and so is her enthusiasm for self-sufficiency. What's left is pretty much pure bitch. This morning she screamed at me because I never run water in my milk glasses before I put them in the sink. "You try and get your hand down in there. Break *your* goddam knuckles."

Charlie calls and Laura won't talk to him. His voice sounds like it's coming from the very top part of his throat only. Laura's in the bedroom, leaning in close to the mirror, picking at her face. My heart beats faster when I see a white T-Bird.

I wake up and Laura is at the window, trying to open it like it's a door. She's saying hold on hold on hold on. Charlie's in the parking lot yelling Laura and something and Laura and something else and Laura and something else again. She's getting all confused in the Venetian blind. I get out of bed, go up behind her and say, "Laura," as softly as I can. She comes to or wakes up or whatever, looks embarrassed and then like she's going to cry, grabs a pair of jeans—my jeans—and steps into them. She moves out the door and a minute later I hear the T-Bird start.

In the morning I go out to the kitchen and Laura and Charlie are sitting at the kitchen table, coked to the gills, and ashamed of themselves for never having gone to bed. I yawn, stretch, clear my throat, and just generally act like I've got one busy day ahead of me. That kind of stuff will make a person who has been up all night feel terrible.

When I get home from work Charlie's car is gone. There are bottles of juice and club soda on the counter. A pot of brown rice with about a hundred different kinds of vegetables in it is on the stove. After a night of drug abuse Laura does penance. She'll take a shower and brush her teeth before she goes to bed. "Good night," she'll call from the bedroom.


The phone rings at 3:27 a.m. It's Charlie's sister, dire-sounding as ever. I wake Laura up. She puts the phone between her ear and the pillow, listens for about ten seconds, then says, "Where is he? Where is he now?" It has to be either jail or the hospital, I think. Laura puts the receiver down and stands up in one motion.

"Charlie broke into a Cumberland Farms store. There was a fifteen-year-old girl with him. What do I do?" She's crying and jiggling one leg. "What the fuck do I do?"

"Don't go, Laura. Don't you go."

"He's in jail," she says, then stands perfectly still with her mouth open.

I want to go over to her and put my arm around her but I know she'll squirm away from me. Whatever's going on between her and him is strong enough to move her out of her bed in her sleep and make her try and open a window as if it were a door. He's in trouble and she thinks her being there will make a difference.

"Will you come with me?"

In the car Laura tells me she's just going to get him through this and then she's getting away from him. She believes what she's saying. I know because she's taking deep breaths between sentences, preparing herself.

# ATHLETES AND ARTISTS

Rhea and Charles were married on a Tuesday night. Charles'
two sons and Rhea's daughter and son-in-law came to the wedding. Rhea wore a blue dress that she knew looked dated but
that she'd long thought of as the absolute most beautiful dress
of all times and wanted to be married in. After the ceremony,
they got in two cars and drove to a small, expensive restaurant
where they had rack of lamb, Rhea's favorite.

"Well, Rhea?"

"Well what?"

"Can I take pictures of you or not?"

"What is it with you and these pictures all of a sudden?"

"It's just something I want to do."

"And what about developing? Have you thought about that?
Are you taking them to the drugstore? Because I'm not."

"I'll use a Polaroid. No developing."

"Did you have to ask permission? Couldn't you just have sprung it on me when I was getting out of the shower?"

"I don't want candids. I want you to pose."

"Is there something weird about this?"

"Nothing weird."

"We'll see, Charles. I guess so. We'll see."

Charles and Rhea knew one another when they were younger and married to other people. Rhea and her ex-husband and Charles and his ex-wife went to the same parties, used the same baby-sitters. Rhea thought Charles, the oldest member of the group and the one with the best job, was smart and serious. Charles thought Rhea danced better than any of the other women. At parties, half-drunk, he'd wait for the commotion that meant Rhea was moving the coffee table, making room for dancing.

Once, when a group of them went to the shore for the day, a woman, one of their circle, lost her bridgework in the ocean and was going to have to sit under an umbrella all day with no front teeth. She cried with her hand over her mouth while her husband yelled about four hundred dollars wasted. Rhea volunteered to drive the woman home. Charles watched their faces as they pulled out. The woman sobbing and shaking her head, Rhea looking left and right.

Twenty years later Charles saw Rhea in a department store, thought instantly of that morning on the beach, and said, "Rhea Tyrone."

"I got it," Charles said. "And three rolls of film. They're not rolls, actually. They're cartridges."

"Let's see. How much?"

"Seventy all together, on sale from a hundred and nine."

When they first talked about getting married, Charles said it would be best to sell both houses and buy a condominium. "A clean start and no yard work." The three or four places they saw looked chintzy to Rhea. "They skimped on this one, Charles," she whispered. "They skimped all over the place."

She decided they should sit down, compare both houses and move into the better of the two. They made lists. Charles had central air. Rhea had an enormous kitchen. They both had six-percent mortgages. Charles had a new driveway, concrete. Rhea had walk-in closets. Charles was in a better neighborhood, which tipped the scales. "Neighborhood is everything," the real estate agent said.

Charles, feeling a little guilty about having won the house competition, watched gratefully while Rhea sold most of his furniture.


"Do you read pornography, Charles?"

"Have you ever seen me read pornography?"

"I thought you might have started. I checked your closet for magazines."

"You didn't happen to see those grey slacks of mine while you were in there, did you?"

"The grey pants are gone. Gone. I thought we'd agreed on that."


Rhea's first marriage blew up. Her husband went to a parents' night at their daughter's school, met Terry's softspoken sixth-grade teacher, and asked for a divorce. All in a month.

After seventeen years, Charles wife screamed and said she was getting out. Charles had stood for a moment, filled with admiration for her outburst. His own rage was so thoroughly under control.

With Rhea, he found moments when all of the vagueness fell away, moments of intense, soothing focus. They'd be in a diner, Rhea ordering, her eyes open wide, the waitress standing off to one side. He'd lean back, watch, and not know what he wanted when it was his turn.

"What about Saturday night?"
"No good. I'm having dinner with Terry."
"Sunday?"
"I can't help feeling this should be a bit more spontaneous."
"Sunday, yes or no?"
"Sunday afternoon, then. Not morning, afternoon."

The morning after the wedding, Rhea got up with Charles and made him coffee. She sat on his lap while he drank it. After he left for work, she walked around the house in bare feet, looking around corners and up at the ceilings.

For a year or so, Rhea got up, made coffee, and sat on Charles' lap or on a chair next to him. He moved quickly in his white shirt and dark tie while she sat still in her rumpled pajamas. Rhea loved her mornings, the conversation and then the quiet.

"Okay. Okay, now. Make as though you're opening the oven."
"Don't take it from behind, Charles. Take it from the front."
"I'll take it both ways."

12

"I'm opening the oven."

"There."

"Let me see it. Give it to me."

"It takes sixty seconds, a minute."

"Here it comes. Oh no."

"What?"

"It's bad, Charles. Look how dark."

"Turn on that light. I'll open the curtains. Okay, back by the stove. Sort of look over your shoulder."

"Like this?"

"Good. Move your—let's see—your left arm down. Look dead at me and don't smile. Look normal with your eyes."

"Take the damn picture."

"One, two . . ."

"Give it to me."


When Charles got out of bed one morning, Rhea woke up just long enough to pull her legs into the warm spot. She opened her eyes a second time when she smelled cologne. He sat on the bed to put on his socks; she moved with the tilt of the mattress until she could feel him through the blankets. He went out of the room for what seemed like a minute or two, came back, then kissed her on the nose and mouth. She tasted coffee and toothpaste.

For Rhea, the new morning routine felt like the old one without the distractions that being fully awake had allowed. Curled in the center of the big bed, in the half-light from the bathroom, she lost the sense of the perimeters of her own body. As her own outline blurred, Charles' became sharper. He seemed even busier. His hair shined. His tie shined. She listened to him try to be quiet.

On days when she slept through the two kisses and woke

13

with a start in the bright quiet room, she felt like a girl who has been ordered to take a nap in preparation for some late-night adult event, and does, only to wake up and think she's slept through the night and missed everything.

"Go wet your head."

"What?"

"Wet your head in the sink. Let's see how it looks."

"Okay, but then that's all."

"All right."

"This reminds me of when I was a teenager, wetting my head in the sink. I don't know why we were always doing that, washing our hair in the kitchen. Get me a towel."

"Don't dry it too much. Let's go into the living room, on the couch."

"I know, light the fire."

"By the time I do that your hair will be dry."

"You're big on this wet hair thing, aren't you?"

On the fourth Saturday of every month, Rhea had lunch or dinner with her daughter. Each drove fifty miles to meet the other. It was Terry, not Rhea, who insisted on the strict once-a-month schedule.

"I'm tired of salad bars," Rhea said. "The whole point of going out to lunch is to have somebody else bring the food to you."

"Come on. It's supposed to be great."

14

Terry took two glass plates out of a cooler and handed one to her mother, who was standing on her tiptoes, trying to get a look at the food.

"Don't put too much lettuce on your plate. You won't have room for anything substantial. I hate salad bars, but I understand them," Rhea said, watching what other people put on their plates. Her eyes moved from the spoon or tongs to the hand, up the arm to the face. At the bread board, she cut enough bread for everyone.

"Mom," Terry said.

"I couldn't help it. It was one of those things like when you get stuck holding the door. The blonde fellow thinks I work here. Did you hear him? 'Sourdough, please.' "

As they sat down, Terry said, "How's Charles?"

"Fine, I think."

"You think?"

"He wants to take pictures of me without my clothes on."

"You're kidding."

"Don't laugh."

"I can't help it."

"Nothing dirty, you understand. Just these sort of around the house things."

"It's kind of touching, actually."

"You think?"

"Well, yeah. I mean, he adores you."

"Mmmm," Rhea said and took a long drink of water.

"If it bothers you, the pictures, don't do it."

"It's not that it bothers me so much as that I just don't understand."

"Come on. It's not exactly whips and chains. You're flattered by it, I can tell."

"No. I was sort of flattered at first. I thought it would be sexy and all. But it's not. I get the feeling it isn't working. He isn't getting what he wanted out of it."

"You're doing it already? I thought we were still at the discussion stage here."

"We have almost a hundred pictures."

"And why does he say he wants to take them?"

"He says it's just something he wants to do, which would be fine. Except he gets this look in his eyes when we're taking them. Like he's trying so hard. You know what it reminds me of? It drove me crazy for a week, but I finally thought of it. It reminds me of the look some of the Olympic athletes had in their eyes when they were interviewed after their events. Didn't matter if they'd won or lost. Like if they'd jumped twenty feet, they needed to jump thirty."

Alone in the car on the way home, Rhea repeated bits of what she'd said to Terry at the restaurant. She took one hand off the steering wheel and gestured with it, palm up, while she talked.

When she got home, Charles was sitting at the kitchen table, the stack of photographs in front of him.

"What were you doing just now? What were you thinking about while you looked at them?"

"How was lunch?"

"Don't ignore the question and don't think. Just answer."

"Rhea, we've been through this."

"We have not. You're not telling me the truth."

"You're upset. We won't take anymore. Forget it."

"I am upset. I'm upset and don't tell me to forget it."

She picked up the first picture in the stack, looked at it closely, then held it against the second.

16

"You're a smart man, Charles. You don't do something as outrageous as this without having some sense of why you're doing it. Now come on."

"Come on what? Rhea, you're beautiful. If I were a painter and wanted to do you in the nude, you'd be thrilled. It's as simple as that. Not everything in the world is complicated."


Charles sat alone in the living room, his arms extended out in front of him, a photograph in each hand. He thought of Rhea as she'd been when she'd come home that afternoon—she'd tried to get him to look her in the eye and her hand had tilted so far it had almost touched her shoulder—and looked at a shot of her standing in front of the refrigerator.

He listened to her get out of bed, walk down the hall, come into the room, and sit down beside him.

"The pictures again, huh?"

Charles rubbed his face with the tips of his fingers, pulling the skin down then pushing it up.

"Just explain to me what it's about."

He looked at her for a moment then said, "Sometimes when I look at you . . . I get such a sense of a picture. Everything is just right, the colors, the lines, the proportions. I wanted to get that, to capture it, to bring it through me and say here it is. But it didn't work. The way you think a painter must paint a picture, a beautiful picture, and everybody loves it and he knows he's failed. Except for may be a crease in the wrist or something he wasn't able to get whatever it was—the particular beauty of the thing—that made him want to paint it in the first place."

Rhea put her slippered feet on the coffee table and stared at the space between them. "Keep talking."

"I don't know how else to explain it."

"Don't try to explain. Just talk about it."

Charles spread his fingers and looked at his open palms.

"Sometimes with you there are moments when about twenty thousand things chink into place, things that the rest of the time are just slightly off. There's a kind of hum to it. I can just take it in without knowing, while it's happening, what's so wonderful about it."

Rhea rocked the upper part of her body in a kind of nod and said, "Remember when we were first married we'd get up together in the morning and have coffee? Then I stopped getting up. I lost the one dose of you sitting next to me, but I got you moving around in the dark. It's better because I'm doing even less to get it. That's something like what you're talking about, isn't it?"

Charles smiled and nodded. "Let's have a drink."

They went into the kitchen where they stood at the counter and drank wine, leaning into each other. Rhea rubbed her forehead against Charles' chest.

When their glasses were empty, they separated and went around the kitchen and living room, turning off lights. As she walked behind him down the hall, Rhea put her hands on Charles' shoulders.

# NOTES

Mary lived in the studio apartment in the front of the house. The day I moved in she invited me over for coffee. She had one of those fans that rotates constantly on a stationary base. We sat there with the door open and the fan going, drinking coffee and talking. She told me she was originally from Chicago. I told her I was looking for a job.

We spent a lot of time together that first week. Afternoons, some evenings. Instead of coffee sometimes we had wine. Once, while I was there, she shaved her legs, sitting right at the kitchen table. After each stroke she cleaned the razor in a bowl of hot water.

Then I got the job in the hotel and Mary started leaving these notes on her door. "I've gone to the library." Or, "It's laundry day again. Don't wait." Sometimes just, "Went out. Be back." I'd come home from work, see one of them on her door, and feel sorry for her while I cooked dinner. She didn't get any visitors.

And then two things happened. One, I found out that sometimes when there was a note on the door Mary was home. I heard her toilet flush. She was supposed to be at a barbecue. And two, people started going in and out of her apartment late at night. I happened to work second shift one night and just as I was pulling into our driveway, the porch light went on. I sat in the car and waited. A man in a black T-shirt walked out carrying a paper bag.

"Drugs," I said. Mary had been out of work for as long as I'd known her and I figured someone had told her it was a good living. Both the notes (I have your money, I'm just not home at the moment) and the three a.m. door openings and closings could easily have been drug-related.

I was satisfied until the Sunday afternoon I saw an elderly man walk up to her door, read the note, smile and turn around. No drug dealer would grin because the person who owed him money was at a garage sale. Just to be sure I called Mary and asked her how many grams there were in an ounce.

"I don't know," she said. "There's eight ounces in a cup, right?"

It wasn't drugs.

A week later I saw Mary sitting on the front steps smoking a cigarette, looking pretty good in a dress and high heels.

"Going somewhere special?" I asked.

"Is that my phone?" she said, getting up.

I followed her inside and sort of stood in her doorway.

"Maybe it was yours?" she said.

Her apartment was cleaner then I'd ever seen it. There were bowls of Fritos on the end tables. I tried to get a conversation going, asked her how she was doing, took a handful of Fritos.

"I have to run to the store," she said, picking up a pencil.

"Gone to the 7-11 for ice," it said.

As far as I could tell there were three men, two teenage girls and a woman with blonde hair in Mary's apartment that night. Prostitution? I could see Mary as this sort of madam, lounging around in her robe telling people what to do. But in a studio apartment? With Fritos?

The notes got longer and more specific. I thought about moving. Mary beat me to it. I looked out of my bedroom window one morning and saw three men carrying furniture out of Mary's apartment and putting it in a van. Mary was not there. I wondered if she'd been murdered. I threw on a pair of shorts and hurried outside.

I caught up with one of them and demanded to know where Mary was.

"You must be the neighbor," he said, shifting the lamp he was carrying from one hand to the other. "Why don't you mind your own business and leave people alone?"

By the time the police got there the men had left and Mary's apartment was empty. I got one of them to call the owner of the building who said that Mary had given him thirty days notice.

"She moved, buddy. That's all," the cop said as he hung up the phone.

He refused to run a check on the license plate number of the van.

About a month later I was downtown and I saw Mary. It was eleven-thirty in the morning and she was coming out of a bar. I wanted to ask her if there was anything I could do but while I was looking for a place to park she disappeared into an office building.

An old man has moved into Mary's apartment. No notes. No noises at night. No big-mouthed blonde-haired women. Just the smell of beef stew and terrible coughing attacks in the morning.

He tries to start conversations with me, about sports mostly. I hardly even answer him when he asks me a question. Like he'll say, "Who do you like in tonight's game?" and I'll say, "What game?" and walk away.

# MEETINGS

"I'll bet you were a lot of fun when you drank."

"I was. Always. A lot of fun."

"I knew it." Ruth stared at the glove compartment and smiled. "And people probably loved it when you came to their parties."

"No. I drank at a bar mostly."

"Oh." She slid down in her seat and looked at Alex. "The same bar all the time? With the same people?"

"Mmmm."

"Then they loved it when you came through the door. I wish I'd known you then."

"Someplace Else, that was the name of the bar." Alex grabbed the steering wheel with both hands. "It was a big room, no windows. You could spend twelve hours in there without even trying. You'd get wrapped up in one thing after another."

"Everything a bar should be."

"More."

The front door of the building Alex and Ruth were sitting in front of opened and a man walked out.

"Max," Alex said. Ruth waved. The man made an exaggerated hat-tipping motion.

"Don't come over here. Please don't come over here," Alex said.

"He's not. He's getting in his car."

They were quiet until the man had started his car and pulled away, and then Alex said, "A stranger would come into the bar, someone none of us knew, and we'd bet on how much money he had in his pocket. We'd write down our guesses on slips of paper and sign them. Then we'd ask him to count his money in front of us. Most people went along with it because what the hell. We'd announce the winner and award prize money. Women won a lot of the time. They were good at it."

Ruth looked at Alex as if he was telling a good story to other people, one that she'd heard already and liked. "I'll bet you were the one to ask the stranger to count his money."

"I was."

"Yep. I could see you introducing yourself and shaking his hand then leaning close while you explained the whole thing to him, acting like it was something you and he had to go along with for the sake of the others."

"Worked every time."

"I know it did."

Ruth looked out her window. "You know when I had my best times? The mornings after. I'd sit around with a couple of girlfriends. We'd drink big bottles of soda and laugh about the night before. One girl always brought dope. She said we had to smoke our hangovers out. As I got high, I'd remember things from the night before and my stomach would clutch. I'd look around at everybody in my pajamas. One would have my robe on over her jeans. Somebody else, my nightgown."

"Do you still see them?"

"When? I see you all the time."

"I don't see the bar people anymore either. No, you know when I saw them? At that wedding. They all know I'm not drinking so they were careful around me. Women kept asking me to dance. One guy offered me a shot and his girlfriend stepped on his foot."

Alex turned on the inside light and looked at his watch. "Do you want to go to the diner?"

"It's a wonder you ever thought to stop drinking, having so much fun."

"The accident, mostly. And I wasn't remembering. You've heard all of this."

Ruth reached up and touched the car ceiling with both hands. "Do you always tell the truth at meetings?" She looked at her spread fingers.

"Yes."

"Always?"

"Yes."

"God, I don't. I mean I start out to, but then as I'm talking I find myself making up little details. Big details. I lie. I feel like my stories don't make enough sense for other people to understand unless I change them around."

"You should just tell them. Nobody's stories make sense. Not *sense* sense."

"Yes they do. They're dramatic. About marriages and lost jobs. Mine are so much less definite. I feel like I have to give them a little shape, a little logic, so I do."

"What about tonight? Eva's story? There wasn't anything dramatic there."

25

"Her. Would you tell me what she's doing at meetings?"

Alex looked down at his lap and laughed.

"I mean," Ruth said. "A glass of wine when she got home from work? 'I had to have that wine. Had to have it.' "

"She never misses a meeting, though."

"Oh, she's very serious. She's like Mary Tyler Moore. I read that she checked into Betty Ford because she had one vodka on the rocks before dinner. One single Stolichnaya. How many people have to have coffee when they get up in the morning? They're not going to meetings."

"They probably could if they wanted to."

"I know, they have them for everything now. There's a support group for women who are in love with priests. I saw the founder interviewed. You'd think they'd have to go national to get enough people for one room. Maybe Eva's going to the wrong meetings. She needs a group. She just doesn't need A.A."

"Or maybe she doesn't tell the truth when she talks."

"Go to hell. You don't either. You never said a word about how much fun you had drinking."

"I'm afraid to. I'll get a ball rolling. Everybody will come up with their favorite drunk story."

"So what? We should talk about it. About how boring it is not to drink sometimes. How you miss it. It's rewarding and all, but it's also a goddamn bore."

"Right. We'll go around once and everybody'll get all misty. Then somebody will suggest going out for a drink."

"Maybe Eva will invite us over for wine and cheese."

Alex leaned over and kissed Ruth between the eyes.

"I wish I hadn't told you about not always telling the exact truth because now when I talk at meetings you're going to think I'm lying and I might not be."

"That's right."

26

"We could start going to separate meetings."

"No. If you go to a new meeting you'll meet another handsome alcoholic."

"And you'll be left with Eva. All right, I'm going to tell the truth from now on. You don't have to worry. If I say it, you'll know it's the truth."

"You're a reformed recovering alcoholic."

"Re-formed."

# WORKING

Mrs. Paterson ate, it seemed to me, too much breakfast for an old lady. She had oatmeal, a boiled egg, toast, juice, coffee, and four stewed plums. I don't know why they were called plums and not prunes. They were certainly wrinkled.

"What is your name?" she said after she'd opened the door that first morning.

"Lawrence."

"All right, then, Lawrence. Come in."

She said Lawrence slowly, with a lot of emphasis on the first syllable, like she didn't believe it was really my name.

I wanted to look like I knew what I was doing. I tried to push the cart into her room. Everything on board rattled. I stopped, picked up the tray, carried it past Mrs. Paterson—she was wearing a floor-length green robe—and put it on the dresser. I went back for the cart, lifted it up and over the doorsill, wheeled it to the dresser, then put the tray back in place.

I kept my eyes on my hands during all of this, sure that

my looking at Mrs. Paterson would bring on the What-The-Hell-Are-You-Doing I could feel in the air. I tried to look as though I'd gone through the same motions a hundred times.

I had the cart moving again before I realized I didn't know where I was going exactly. The table seemed like the logical place for a person to eat, but it was all the way on the other side of the room. To get to it I would have had to pass the large unmade bed. I didn't think I should do that.

"What is the matter with you? Keep going. Do you want me to eat standing up?"

The table it was, then. I pushed towards it.

"Now where are you going? Stop. I sit on one corner of the bed and eat. This corner," she said and pointed.

I maneuvered the cart to within a foot of the bed then turned it on the diagonal so she could slip in behind it.

"Stop fidgeting with it."

I stood up straight.

"Look at my hands."

I did. They looked like regular old-lady hands to me.

"Arthritis. I'm full of it. I can't grip."

She looked at the tray. I thought she was going to tell me I had to feed her.

"I can't open that packet of jelly. Or the creamer for my coffee. And I see we've added a new horror." She picked up the foil-sealed juice cup. "Open this too. And the sugar packets, four of them."

I wanted to wash my hands before I put them all over her breakfast.

"Let's go."

I tore the tops off the sugar packets.

"Stand them up against the saucer."

I opened the jelly.

"Mixed fruit, tell them for tomorrow. No grape."

The creamer gave me trouble. By the time I'd broken through the foil and paper top, the plastic bottom was so dented it wouldn't stand up on the tray.

"Give it to me."

I couldn't see anything else that needed opening. The oatmeal was accessible enough, as were the plums.

"Okay?" I said.

"No. Take the top off the egg. Just the top. I want the bottom whole."

I tapped the egg with a teaspoon then took off a little cap of shell.

"Okay?"

"Pour the coffee. and make sure you're the one who brings me my breakfast tomorrow. I can't go through a training session every day."

I nodded and poured, understanding that it was going to be me every morning for the next three weeks and that, short of quitting, there was nothing I could do about it. I turned to go, feeling myself at the beginning of a very bad time.

"And don't forget about the jelly. Mixed fruit, I want."


I was chosen to handle Mrs. Paterson's room service because I was bottom bellhop. The other two were older and had worked for the hotel during previous summers. I was new. It was my first job.

I wanted to work hard and get paychecks, to join my parents who I'd watched go off in the morning, freshly showered, and come back at night, rumpled and paler. When my mother called from work her voice sounded different, a little embarrassed but also show-offy. You could tell there were other people listening. My father had this way of exhaling before he picked up his fork, as though eating his dinner was the final thing he had to do that day.

I thought working would be hard in a clean sort of way, like running as far as you can. But it wasn't. My insides lurched and then stopped and shook at work.

Bellhops were beneath busboys who were beneath waiters and so on, which made me the lowest of all. I never pushed the swinging door of the employee lounge—it was a smoke-filled hallway—without heart-pounding terror. On my way to work I'd rehearse what I wanted to sound like an offhand greeting, then berate myself for rehearsing. In the lounge, I'd go directly to the rack of bellhop jackets where I'd flip through the available candidates as if I was shopping, and not very hopefully. I'd put one on, button it, then tug at the collar and sleeves. Those red jackets, grease-stained and faded, fit no one.

When I'd pulled and rebuttoned as long as I felt I could, I'd go and stand near the other bellhops. There was Ricky and there was Lou. Ricky was blonde with all these muscles and a handsome face. He looked like he could step easily away from the silly red jacket. Lou was dark, oily, and antsy. He was always bobbing around Ricky, gesturing wildly. He talked about Marty a lot, the kid who had had my job the previous summer. Marty had stolen porterhouse steaks from the walk-in freezer. Marty had bought a pot from the chef and called California from what had once been a banquet manager's office. I didn't want to do any of those things. I wanted to bellhop. I knew I was a disappointment to them, to Lou anyway. There'd been an opening and instead of a Marty he'd gotten me.

So there went the clean of how I hoped work would be. And the hard part wasn't much better. There wasn't enough for bellhops to do. There were days, a lot of days, when not a single suitcase went up or came down.

With no luggage to carry, we did whatever Mr. Conly, the manager, told us to do. When the lifeguard didn't show up—he was nineteen, I remember, and married—we vacuumed the pool and stacked towels. Most of the guests were too old to want to swim. We'd get an occasional lady who'd make her way across the shallow end, being careful to keep her head out of the water.

When there weren't enough busboys in the dining room, we were called. In the oak-panelled world of The Bounty, stand-ins who didn't know where the butter pats were kept and couldn't properly fold a napkin, were nothing but in the way.

Sometimes we worked in the kitchen. We'd be put in front of a vat of carrots or onions and told to peel. We'd go for hours, peeling carelessly.

Then there was painting the boat. The yacht that Eisenhower used when he was president was permanently docked in the bay behind the hotel. It was supposed to be a tourist attraction, but I never saw anybody go and look at it. You'd expect a president's yacht to be luxurious. This thing was ordinary. It had little foam rubber cushions on the couch and chairs. Even with the presidential seal, it looked like something you'd buy secondhand.

When we were told to paint a man named Edward in maintenance would give us a coffee can of protective oil and a brush apiece. We'd start anywhere and keep putting the stuff on until Mr. Conley came out to the dock and waved us in.

If it was raining or Mr. Conley thought the boat needed time to dry between coats—he seemed to think we were out there putting complete coats on the thing—we'd be stationed in the lobby in case of walk-ins, guests without reservations. I'd stand by a window and look out into the parking lot.

33

I first heard about Mrs. Paterson in the employee lounge.

"Miserable," a waiter said, looking into his coffee and giggling. "Every year I say she can't possibly have lived through another winter and every year she does. Ricky, you know, she gets room service in the morning. One of your guys has to do it."

Lou said, "Lawrence."

Ricky smiled or had been smiling throughout, I'm not sure which, and said, "Lawrence can do it."

It was being identified as one of Ricky's guys that got me. I accepted immediately. I didn't know that Mrs. Paterson was always given to the boob bellhop.


Every morning for the next three weeks I went first to the lounge to get a jacket, then to the kitchen for Mrs. Paterson's cart. Hers was always the only room service going out. The other guests could barely afford breakfast in the dining room.

I liked watching Gus, the breakfast cook, prepare the tray. He worked quickly, slamming pans onto burners and kicking drawers closed. On the third day he said, "Hey, com'ere." I took a step towards him—we were only about five feet apart to begin with. He handed me three pieces of warm bacon. He gave me something every day after that. A half an English muffin. A shrimp.

I hated to see him drop the plums into their white bowl because that meant it was time for me to head off to room 304. As I made my way along the halls—the cart had one uncooperative wheel—I wanted both to hurry so as to lessen my chances of having to roll grinning past Ricky and Lou, and to go slow to put off Mrs. Paterson. She'd gotten meaner.

Before her, the only contact I'd had with old ladies had

been with my grandmothers. I had two. They were nice old ladies, not just to me but to everybody, especially if you were a kid and they thought my parents were kids. They called them that, the kids. There was an old lady at school too. She was just a little cranky. Nothing like Mrs. Paterson. I felt like telling her, "Hey, I'm a boy."

One morning during the second week of Mrs. Paterson, I knocked on her door and got no response. I knocked again and heard a faint groan. "Oh God," I thought, "she's on the bathroom floor and can't get up." I ran and got a maid who used her passkey to open the door.

Mrs. Paterson was safe in bed. When she saw the maid she pulled the sheet up to her chin.

"I can't get up."

"Why not?" I said and heard the maid leave.

"You put so damn much salt in the food, I'm all swollen. Tell the cook he can't make bad food good by salting it to death. My poor ankles."

She'd always been up and washed by the time I got there. She'd had her robe on and her hair in place. She looked so much worse, lying there with one foot sticking out. Her toes were pushed together like she had invisible pointy shoes on. Her toenails were yellow and many-layered like slate.

"What do you want me to do?"

"I want you to get over here right now and help me. I want you to get my robe and slippers. I want my food before it's ice cold."

I saw one slipper on the floor and kneeled down to look for the other. There it was, lying on its side. I wanted to throw it at her—the stupid ugly slipper—and run away from the smell

35

of sleep and urine. But I couldn't. My sense of duty, my obedience to adults, my gut fear of Mrs. Paterson all came together and settled over me.

I pulled the covers off her, keeping my arm rigid, not knowing what I'd see next. Men's pajamas, they looked like. I put the slippers on her feet. "Come on, sit up," I said. She just looked at me with her head hanging to one side. Who said she could care so little about how she looked to me? I was a bellhop not a doctor.

I put my hands under her arms and tried to slide her up the headboard. She started making whimpering noises, then in her normal voice said, "My robe, Lawrence."

I got the robe, put her arms in it, moved her feet to the floor and sat her up. I kneeled to put one piece of the robe's zipper into the other. I pulled the ring past her knees, groin, belly, and breasts. Up near her chin I gave it an extra tug.

"There are only three sugars here. Go get me another."

I turned, walked out of the room, and went down to the kitchen. I got Mrs. Paterson that sugar and went back up to her room. I tore and peeled and cracked the plastic and packets and egg. When I'd finished I joined Ricky and Lou who were peeling cucumbers. After I'd done a couple I started to feel that if I'd handled Mrs. Paterson differently from the start, if I'd been tougher, she wouldn't be pulling this on me.

"How's Mrs. Paterson treating you?" Lou asked, figuring he'd get something to laugh at until the cucumbers were done.

"All right," I said.


Getting a maid to open the door became part of my routine, but I always knocked first. Just as I'd become adept at getting the tray primed for her, I was soon able to have her robed and slippered in a matter of seconds. She complained constantly while I was in the room. I heard her the way you hear traffic when you're walking on a highway.

She had lunch and dinner in the dining room. If we'd been assigned there I'd see her at her table, always the same one. She'd call me over, ask for a magazine or tell me to grind pepper on her baked potato. Once I brought her a glass of water and she said it was too big.

"I asked you for water, Lawrence. I didn't mean a pitcherful."

"Drink what you want and leave the rest," I said because Lou was at the next table, pretending to fill the salt shaker.

"No. Take this away and dump half of it out."


On Mrs. Paterson's last morning, I burned my tongue on a sausage Gus had given me. I put an ice cube in my mouth before I left the kitchen, but it had melted by the time I got to the elevator. My tongue hurt so much and I was on my way to stink and abuse. I kicked the cart, but carefully not savagely like I needed to. I thought about mashing the two pieces of toast together, pouring juice in the oatmeal.

I looked at the plums. I knew they'd be cold because Gus always took them out of a small refrigerator at his feet. I lifted one out of the syrup, put it in my mouth, and pushed my tongue into the cold insides. It soothed the burn instantly but was so sweet it tasted almost rotten.


"I'm missing a plum, Lawrence. Four plums, I take. Not three."

"There are no more."

37

"Don't be stupid. Go down and get me another one."

"There are no more. No more. I checked already."

She looked at me and I swear I saw her face give just a little.

"Get out. Let me eat in peace."


So as not to have to carry her luggage, I stayed out of the lobby as much as I could that day. When I was sure she'd gone—I stood at a third-floor window and watched Lou and Ricky carry her pink suitcases—I went to the front desk and asked if there was a tip for me from room 304. The clerk handed me an envelope that had Lawrence Bellhop written in pointy script across the front of it. I wanted twenty dollars. There was fifty inside. With the money in my hand and Mrs. Paterson in the taxi, it all seemed worth it.

# BACK IN THE DAYS

I was nineteen and thought I was colorful because I got drunk a lot and slept with just about anybody who offered. I wanted people to think I was happy-go-lucky, reckless. I wanted to be a beautiful psychotic like Judy Garland or Zelda Fitzgerald.

I was working in a highway bar where the customers were mostly middle-aged singles. I enjoyed the grittiness of the place, felt happily cut off from the world I'd grown up in.

The bar had been popular with organized crime figures at one time. Someone told me an FBI agent used to sit in the parking lot taking pictures. The only Mafia types I was able to find there were men with Italian last names and noses who were involved in some mysterious way with controlling the area's garbage pick up. These garbage men were always ordering things that weren't on the menu. They once threw a lavish party for one of their own on the night before he was to turn himself in for extortion. The heads of drug and prostitution rings had, I guess, found nicer places to hang out.

Two men owned the bar. One was fat and friendly and a slob. The other was a handsome Greek who used to take women upstairs and have sex with them in the storeroom. The two owners didn't talk to each other, at all. The story went that they had once been like brothers but as the business had grown so had the tension between them. They had begun having fierce arguments. Eventually they'd just stopped talking. They worked side by side in the kitchen and never once, that I saw, did either one say a word to the other. Finally one of them walked out and I never saw him again. The other one, the slob, had the locks changed.

I used to work until two in the morning and then I'd sit at one end of the bar with some of the waitresses and bartenders and drink until five or six. The other employees my age, a couple of nursing students, hardly ever stayed to drink, and when they did they had one glass of sangria and then went home to study or to sleep.

There was one older guy, a bartender, who one night showed me a picture of himself when he was twenty-one. Even though I thought he looked moon-faced in it, I told him that he'd been a very handsome young man. After that he took the picture out of his wallet to show other people every time I went near him so I was obligated to say how nice-looking I thought he'd been all over again.

One afternoon he and I were getting ready to go on and we passed each other in the kitchen. It was one of the holidays, I forget which, Easter Sunday maybe. He said "Happy Easter, honey." While he kissed me he tried to stick his tongue in my mouth. After that I was careful not to flirt with him anymore. I wasn't completely without standards.

I was living with my sister and her five-year-old son. He was not allowed to come into my room before noon. At twelve o'clock exactly he'd open the door and stick his head in to see if I was awake. I usually was and still drunk from the night before; I'd let him climb up on the bed. We'd laugh and talk until we'd get into an argument and then he'd storm out, his big hard shoes stomping down the hall.

I'd get up and go to the kitchen for some juice and a vitamin pill and to tell my sister about the night before. She had just separated from her husband. By exaggerating my misadventures I was saying to her, "See? This is what's waiting for you in the wonderful world of singlehood. Maybe you'd better reconsider. So what if he can't hold a job."

I was making a lot of money which I used to further my reputation as a silly person. I claimed that when I was in a department store I felt compelled to spend every dime I had with me. The trouble was I bought isolated beautiful things— a silk nightgown that I loved to smoke in, a red belt you could hardly feel between your fingers—so I never looked too great.

I used to lose money a lot too. I think now that some of it was probably stolen by the people whose hands were groping around in the vicinity of my back pockets. At the bar we used to split tips which meant I got my money in one lump sum at the end of the night. I was always too impatient to open my pocketbook, take out my wallet, open it up, and put the money away, so I just used to slip the eighty or ninety or a hundred bucks in my back pocket.

I spent a lot of money on food; I was always trying to cure hangovers by eating big rich lunches. We lived across the street from a Shop-Rite. I'd go over there and buy anything that caught my eye. I wanted to make a perfect cheesesteak. I bought a piece of filet mignon. My sister was horrified.

41

What about sex, you're saying to yourself. She said she had sex with anybody and all we've seen her do so far is run away from an old man in a restaurant kitchen and have her buttocks massaged by thieves. Two incidents stand out in my memory. One has to do with a handsome young man who patterned himself on the Greek owner. He drove a Porsche with plaid seats. He sat down next to me at the bar one night. I was flattered by his choice of stools so I tried to get a conversation going. He'd just been dumped by the girl who had insisted he buy the Porsche. I found his pain exciting. We went to a motel and I got on top and did most of the work. When he finally came, which took forever, he said the name of the Porsche-girl, Linda. I felt sort of Christian about the whole thing, like a missionary bringing relief to someone who was suffering.

The other took place after an athletic night spent in the bed of a person who asked to be called Crazy. I was scurrying around looking for my purse, eager to get the hell out of there and home to my nephew and my juice, when he introduced me to his stern-looking business-suited roommate as Valerie, the name of a girl who had been at our table the night before and who Crazy had tried before he'd tried me.

So what did I learn from all of this? If I'm no longer living this way, what was the turning point? What grizzly thing happened that got me safely into A.A. or college or an exclusive relationship?

The son of the people who owned the cabinet store next door to my apartment told me that he was absolutely, unalterably in love with me. We came in contact as a result of my ongoing battle with my car, which was forever breaking down. He brought an umbrella outside while I waited in the rain for a tow truck. He suggested mechanics.

I quit my job at my parents' request and with their money

went to St. Croix for a week. I planned to spend my time walking on the beach and thinking. My first day there I went on a snorkeling excursion—physical fitness was part of the plan—and got badly sunburned. The remaining five days I spent in my room putting vinegar, which I could get only by ordering a green salad from room service, on my scorched skin. I couldn't wait to heal, to go home, to get back to my fledgling relationship with the cabinetmaker.

Bob became my official boyfriend. We went to the movies a lot. One evening we were walking back to the apartment after having seen a real good one and one of my old buddies passed us in a big white car. He blew the horn and waved. I went to wave back but the hand I raised had Bob's hand in it and he wasn't letting go. I looked like the referee at a prize fight when he holds the winner and still champion's gloved hand in the air.

I made dinner for Bob almost every night. After all of those hangover lunches, I knew how to handle myself in the kitchen.

As I settled into domesticity, my sister started going out a lot. I was the one who made coffee in the morning and cleaned out the cabinet under the sink. She giggled over escapades and bought nice underwear.

After a year of magnificent dinners, Bob left me for a younger woman he called Sues or Suze. His mother, who worked with him in the cabinet store, was greatly relieved. Early on she'd told him that she'd seen me walk out of my apartment and into the street in my nightgown, which I don't remember ever doing.

I was left with all of the kitchen utensils I'd accumulated, with a paunch, and without the energy to go back to sleeping around. And anyway, the New Right was coming into its own.

Even Cosmo was telling us to make them earn it. I'd done my part for the sexual revolution so I figured I should get it on this one too. My sister, another woman of the times, has reunited with her husband. They bought a house and a car and they're buying furniture like crazy.

# POLLYANNA

When the boss sent out a memo about the Christmas party, New Anne—we still called her that even though Old Anne had long since retired—said, "Where I used to work we had a Pollyanna." Most of us stopped typing. "Yeah," she said. "You put all of the names in a hat then everybody picks one out and buys a present for that person."

"No," Evelyn, the typist who had been there the longest, said without looking up. Evelyn was a Fundamentalist. She had bits of the scriptures taped to her stapler and pencil cup. She didn't approve of New Anne who wore low-cut sweaters and didn't wear pantyhose a lot of the time.

"Come on," New Anne said. She began to cut sheets of paper into rectangles with the scissors that were chained to her desk. "This gives you something to do at the party. Everybody buys funny things, things that fit the personality of the person."

"I do not need to add any names to my shopping list,

45

thank you," Bart the office manager said. He'd worked for the company for twenty-nine years. Everybody hated him. He sat right behind me and was constantly talking on the phone to doctors about his elbow, his eardrum, or his dog Munchkin. The conversations were detailed and horrible and he said doctor a lot. "Yes, Doctor. Very good, Doctor. Thank you for taking the time to return my call, Doctor." The doctor, doctor, doctors bothered me more than the descriptions of accumulating yellowish fluids.

Bart should have kept his mouth shut about the Pollyanna. People were for it all of the sudden, just for the sake of being against him.

"Let's do it," Chuck said. He was the account rep with the highest sales figures. We'd all heard a rumor that he was going to be made Vice President of Sales in the spring.

Evelyn, who I think harbored a pretty strong lech for Chuck even though she acted like she thought he was just a nice kid, said, "Yeah, it sounds like a lot of fun."

"It's a terrific icebreaker," New Anne said by way of welcoming Evelyn aboard the bandwagon.

Things went that way for Chuck. People liked him. He was the office bad boy. When he got a phone call he'd pick up the receiver and say, "Chuck Taylor, what can I do you for?" His clients loved it. And he had a habit of letting his shirttail hang out of his pants in the back. It made him look busy. The new salesmen were starting to let the backs of their shirts come out of their pants some afternoons.

Bart's clothes were good quality and always neat. Once I heard him say that unless your tie had a dimple right under the knot, you weren't properly dressed.

"You have to ask Mr. George about this," Bart said, looking from Chuck to Evelyn to New Anne. "He wants the Christmas party to be elegant this year. I know, I heard him say it. I don't think this qualifies as elegant."

The mention of Mr. George slowed the Pollyanna's momentum. Chuck, who didn't deserve his reputation as a rip, said, "If Mr. George doesn't want it, we won't do it. No big deal."

"Who wants to ask him?" New Anne said. She wanted to make it clear that even though it had been her idea, she wasn't doing the asking.

"Why don't you do it, Chuck?" Bart said, smiling and looking towards Mr. George's door. "Go right in."

"I'll mention it to him," Chuck said. "When he comes by."

Ordinarily Mr. George came out of his office every hour or so. He'd walk around, get a drink at the fountain, smile at people. That afternoon, though, an hour and a half went by, then two, and no Mr. George. Finally, after two hours and fifty minutes, the door opened. Chuck stood up.

"Some of the girls were wondering if it would be all right with you if we had—what's it called?—a Pollyanna at the Christmas party."

"What?"

"A Pollyanna. Pick names out of a hat and each buy a present for one person."

"Fine."

Mr. George headed for the water fountain then stopped and looked around. Everybody was staring at him.

"Was there something else?"

Bart piped up. "No, Mr. George. Nothing else. I just thought we should okay this gift-giving thing with you before we went ahead with it is all."

And so the squares of paper went into a pale green dish

that Evelyn kept on her desk, loaded with Jolly Rancher candies. A lot of times on my back from the bathroom, I'd wanted a red one. I could have asked Evelyn for it except that I never saw her eat one. Those candies just stayed in their dish until they didn't seem like food anymore; they seemed like office supplies.

People drew according to rank. Chuck and Bart both expected to go first and met head on, the green dish between them. In a monstrously benevolent move, Chuck let Bart draw first.

When it came around to my turn Bart the blackball was still in the dish. I hesitated before I picked, changing my mind at the last second. I opened my square and saw a giant first letter B and an a, r, and t. "Bart," I said. I heard a snicker and the sounds of puffs of air being let out through noses. I looked over at Bart. He was standing near his desk, smiling and fidgeting with the knot in his tie.

"Get him something mean," Evelyn whispered.

"Get him nothing," somebody else said to the back of my neck.


A couple of days after the drawing Bart left for a week's vacation in the Florida Keys. He drove down in a rented car (full-size, he told all of his callers, full-size) with his dog. There was a lot of talk about how great it was not to have him around. We took turns using his typewriter which was better than anybody else's. It had a memory.

I was thinking about the present I had to buy. I knew people were counting on me to come through with something nasty. I thought about going to one of those pharmacies that have walkers and bedpans in the windows and getting him something medicinal.

"Do one of those things, a box inside a box inside a box, then don't put anything inside the last box," the mail clerk said.

In the bathroom, New Anne leaned towards the mirror, drew a thin line of maroon above her upper lip with a tiny brush, said she'd get him a case of Grecian Formula, then watched herself laugh. When she'd stopped laughing she started on her lower lip.


About midway through Bart's vacation week, I was watching the national news and a thing came on about a heat wave in south Florida. The temperature in the Keys, the reporter said, had gone above a hundred three days in a row. I thought about Bart down there in his seersucker suit, expecting eighties during the day and a chill at night.

He came back to work with sunburned cheeks. Right away Chuck asked him how his vacation was. "Warm," he said. "Very warm."

It was not good to have him back. I realized what a relief it had been not to have him sitting up straight in his chair behind me, looking over my shoulder. When I got up to go to lunch, the back of my chair slammed into his desk. He cleared his throat and kept clearing it until I was out of the room.

Almost all of his phone conversations started with talk about Florida. "Yes, there was that heat wave . . . very, very hot, but Key West was charming. So tropical. People keep lizards as pets—bigger than Munchkin and some of them on leashes. After dinner we sat on the beach and watched the sun set."

49

I steeled myself for a couple of weeks of Bart telling his clients and their secretaries about sunsets and leashes. But as the days passed his phone talk changed. Pretty soon he was trashing the whole trip. "Horrible. A complete waste of vacation time. The heat was so intense I was afraid to take Munchkin out in it and she wouldn't stay in the room by herself without crying. I ate all of my meals sitting on the bed."

Either the vacation had been awful and he hadn't wanted to admit it right away, or there had been good moments but at home he was better at complaining so he complained. Thinking about it made me aware of him there behind me. I turned around. He looked at me, opened his eyes wide, and sucked in his cheeks. "Yes?" he said.


The Christmas party was two days off and I still hadn't bought the present. I'd gone to gift shops. I'd made lists. I'd looked in the backs of magazines. I'd thought about all of the gifts I'd ever gotten and which ones I'd liked. When I found myself walking around my apartment hoping to find something that looked new enough to give him, I took my Visa card out from underneath the tray in the silverware drawer, put it in my wallet, and took a bus downtown.

I went first to a men's store and walked up and down the aisles. It was crowded and everybody seemed to be buying for somebody they knew well.

I went to a gourmet store. The smell of coffee and yeast perked me up. People there all looked like they were buying for coworkers. Or for their doormen. Maybe for the guy who cuts their hair. I should have bought something right away. The longer I stayed, the harder it got. I made it almost to the cash register with a glass coffee pot that came with my choice of three exotic blends, then I remembered I'd never seen Bart drink coffee. The rest of us went through pot after pot but he never had any. I put the box back on the shelf and walked out.

I wanted to get on the bus and go home. I'd reached a point of indecision it's difficult to come back from. I'd fallen into the rhythm of walking and looking and didn't feel able to stop and buy.

Shopping-numb, and not paying attention, I stepped onto a grate and got hit by a burst of hot, wet, food-smelling air. With the steam on my legs and the cold air on my face, I thought about Bart on vacation, sweating or not sweating, eating cheese and crackers in his room or a piece of fresh tuna in the open air. I kept walking.

Some of the stores I passed had closed for the night. I'm staying, I told myself, until the last one turns off its lights and goes home.

*Petcetera, the finest in pet accessories,* the sign, black lettering on a white background, said. They had everything in there. Hats and coats. Brushes and combs. Chairs, pillows, and beds. They had a watercooler a dog could operate. I asked to see a small blue silk quilt. The woman behind the counter said it was a scaled-down version of a really good comforter.


Bart came to the party wearing a tuxedo. A tuxedo. As he unwrapped his gift, he looked all ready to be a good sport. He opened the box and then the tissue paper, lifted the blanket up, and said, "What is it?"

"It's for Munchkin," I said.

"Oh. Oh, good."

51

Chuck was standing right behind him, smiling and rocking back and forth on his heels, a mug of beer in his hand. Later he got drunk and sang *New York, New York* with the band. Bart sat very close to Mr. and Mrs. George and watched.

# TEETH AND NAILS

A young woman walked past Mike and his father, dropped a faded cloth pocketbook on the counter, and said, "Can you tell me what you do with the dead cats?"

"I beg your pardon?" the man behind the counter said.

Mike and his father waited to see if she'd say it again.

"The cats. I know this sounds real bizarre, but it's not. I'm a taxidermist and I want to do a cat. Can I buy a dead one?"

"I don't know. Nobody ever asked before. Let me check with my supervisor."

Looking at the back of the woman's head, Mike's father said, "If you want a dog, why don't you spend a couple of bucks and get something decent? Anything you get here's guaranteed full of worms."

The woman put her hand to her mouth and called, "Excuse me. Before you go can you tell me if the bodies are in good shape?"

"They're fine, perfect. We kill by injection. I'll just be a minute."

Mike said, "I got Tony here, Dad, and he's fine."

"Tony. Jesus, I hate it when people name dogs people names. Can you tell me what you did when you had somebody over the house named Tony? You walk into a guy's house and his dog has the same name as you."

"The kids named him."

The woman turned around, smiled at Mike, and said, "I want a dead cat."

Mike's father leaned in to get a look at her face. "Yeah?" he said. "Terrific. We want a live dog. Come on, Mike. Let's see what's here."

"What do you want with a dead cat?" Mike said.

His father headed off towards the rows of turquoise cages.

"I'm a taxidermist. Well, actually I'm a jeweler, but I'm getting into taxidermy. I love cats. They're so independent. I'd love to do one. What do you do?"

"I'm unemployed since May. You need a practice cat, then?"

"Exactly. I just finished my first squirrel. He's a composite made from three different squirrels, all hit by cars. I never kill anything or anything. Was that your father?"

Mike nodded. "He thinks if he's not here to supervise I'll bring home a Great Dane."

"You live with him?"

"For now."

"For now?"

"I just separated from my wife."

The man behind the counter said, "Okay. She's not sure but she thinks there might be a health regulation forbidding the sale of dead animals. God knows we could use the money. Anyway, she said you should check back in a couple of days."

54

"Thank you. I will." The woman picked up her pocketbook, leaned back against the counter, and said, "What did you do before you were unemployed?"

"Taught college. American history."

"Really? I always liked history, especially the Civil War."

"My specialty."

"Why'd you stop?"

"I was fired."

"Oh. Sorry."

"No."

"You didn't like it?"

"Teaching was all right, but I used to sit in my office and imagine I could hear the administration digging tunnels under my chair. It was a relief when the floor finally gave way."

"Like gophers, huh?"

"More like cave miners. Do you want to go with me tonight?"

"I'd like to, but I can't. I'm giving this party. Why don't you come?"


The door was opened by a fat middle-aged woman who was on the phone. "Come on in," she said, the receiver on her shoulder. "You must be Mike. I'm Emily. Janey should be right down." She took the telephone into a brightly lit bathroom and closed the door.

There were platters of hors d'oeuvres on the counters and table. On a shelf above the sink there was a small stuffed lizard. Its eyes had been replaced by red stones. A triangular piece of hammered gold stuck out of its open mouth.

"The first piece I ever finished," Janey said. "A former pet." She was wearing a white cotton dress and looked prettier

55

in the kitchen than she had in the pound. "Did you find the house okay?"

"No problem. I used to live around here."

Mike handed her the two pounds of apricots he'd decided on over Mexican beer. They were ripe, out-of-season, and expensive.

"These are beautiful," she said, peering into the bag. "They remind me of cheeks," She put a handful in the middle of a plate of soft cheeses that was on the table.

"Have you lived here long?"

"About three years. It's Emily's house. You met Emily, right?" Janey said looking around.

"She's in there," Mike said, looking toward the closed bathroom door. "You're roommates?"

"We live together, but we're not roommates."

"Oh," Mike said, nodding. "What are you?"

"Emily and I have been together for a long time, forever. I go out with men too, though. I always have," Janey said.

"You should have told me at the pound."

"No. You wouldn't have come."

The bathroom door opened.

"Don't look so guilty, Mike," Emily said. "You want a beer?"

She took two bottles of dark beer out of the refrigerator and motioned for Mike to sit down. Janey went to the counter and began arranging pieces of raw broccoli and cauliflower on a silver tray. Mike watched her for a moment, trying to detect signs of awkwardness in her movements. There were none. She might have been alone as she alternated the green and white vegetables.

"Janey said you teach American history?"

56

"Taught American history. I lost my job in May."

Emily ran her thumbnail through the label on her beer bottle.

Janey carried the finished platter and a bowl of beige dip into the living room.

"Put ashtrays around in there," Emily called after her, then put her hand on Mike's forearm.

"No sense being angry. I see you looking at her like you expect her to be worried about it. Forget it. Janey doesn't give a damn about other people. I don't mean that exactly. She just sort of drifts through her day, bumping into people and smiling. Ask her and she'll tell you she has all these emotional needs that can't be met by any one person. Bullshit. It's a response she's figured out over the years and likes." Emily gestured toward the living room with her thumb and said, "She has no needs."

Mike put his beer bottle to his lips and swallowed several times. He felt as though he should wonder why Emily was telling him all of this. But he didn't wonder at all. He just wanted to hear whatever she had to say.

"I love her so I put up with it."

The doorbell rang and Emily got up to answer it.

By eleven o'clock there were about forty people at the party. Mike sat in the kitchen talking to a woman in her fifties who was a law student, but he kept his eye on Janey. Her white dress made her easy to spot. He watched her kiss a bald man on the lips. She sent a teenaged boy to the store for more ice. While the law student described the way professional ethics were taught, Janey was persuaded to jitterbug. When he lost sight of her, he excused himself to go look for her.

He found her sitting alone on the stairs.

"Come on," she said. "I want to show you my studio."

He followed her up the stairs, his eyes on the slope of her rear end. At the end of the hall, she opened the door to what should have been the master bedroom.

It smelled like a high school biology lab. Sheets with a faded floral print covered most of the floor. Spools of plastic thread the size of peanut butter jars stood on a plywood workbench under a bright light.

Janey picked up a stuffed squirrel that was curled like a sleeping cat.

"This is my squirrel."

"I never saw one asleep."

"I know. Neither did I. That's why I need the cat. If I get one, I'll position her like this and put her on the rocking chair downstairs. You just can't get the same effect with a squirrel."

In the strong light, Mike was able to see a faint scar below Janey's nose that distorted the outline of her lip.

"Feel how heavy he is." She handed him the squirrel. He leaned back, not wanting to touch it. It fell to the floor.

"I'm sorry," Mike said, kneeling slowly to pick it up.

Janey leaned over and kissed him on the mouth. As he straightened up, he wanted to pull her close, but the squirrel— its weight distracting in his hand—was between them. As much as the kiss was hindered by the squirrel, it was helped by Janey's being taller than Mike's wife: his neck was bent at a pleasantly unfamiliar angle.

Janey turned her head, abruptly ending the kiss. She walked over to a tall stool, the only one in the room, and sat down. Mike put the squirrel down on the workbench.

"You having a good time at the party?"

"Fine. I was talking to that woman who's in law school, Mary somebody."

"She's Emily's friend. Emily's a new lawyer."

"I like her, Emily, but I can't help feeling a little sorry for her."

"Feeling sorry? Emily doesn't need you feeling sorry for her."

"No, I know."

"I hate that. Feeling sorry. People think they're doing you a big favor. But in order to feel sorry for somebody, you first have to think, God, I wouldn't be in his shoes for anything."

Mike walked over to Janey and took her hand. He was about to kiss her again when she said, "Would you mind going downstairs? I feel like working. I'll be down in a while."

Mike stepped back and dropped Janey's hand. His eyes had been closed, moving in for the kiss, and he knew Janey had seen that. "Oh. Oh, okay. I guess I'll see you in a little while, then."

On his way down the stairs, Mike missed a step and arrived in the living room squatting, one leg tucked under, the other sticking straight out in front.

He recovered in a single movement and walked to the picnic table bar, which was again without ice. Two women came over to check on his condition; they thought he was drunk. He told them he was fine, poured scotch into a wine glass, and drank it in one swallow.

He closed his eyes and was glad Janey hadn't seen him fall. He knew she had dismissed him. He felt flushed and a little sick. He didn't know what he was supposed to have done up there. Whatever it was, he thought, must have been something pretty damn exciting. He thought of her sitting cross-legged on the floor of her studio, examining some bit of fur.

He chased the scotch with water scooped out of the penguin-shaped ice bucket and decided to leave. On his way through

59

the empty kitchen, he stopped and slipped the stuffed lizard into his jacket pocket.

He drove to his wife's house. It looked secure, dark and closed, except that one trash can was lying on its side, wet garbage spilling out of the torn plastic bag.

With habitual irritation, he got out of the car, walked to the curb, and carefully uprighted the can. He stooped to pick up a steak bone that had escaped, then wiped his hands on the damp grass. Satisfied, he got back in his car which he'd left running with the defrost on full. The dry heat made him squint.

He parked on the street in front of his father's house. As he went up the stairs, he felt how well his body knew the rhythm of the climb. He knew just where to put his foot on each step in anticipation of the next.

The kitchen light was on. His father had trouble sleeping through the night and would often, after a few hours in bed, sit drinking tea until morning.

"Hey,"

"You home?"

"I'm home."

"Do the chain. I got in bed and couldn't remember if I'd put the chain up or not. I had to get up and check. Sure enough, I'd locked you out."

"Where's Chester?"

"I never saw anything like it. You'd think he lived here all his life. He ate two cans of food, walked around a little, not too much, then planted himself on the rug in the parlor. Dead asleep since ten o'clock. That's one old dog. He's no seven or eight like that guy told us. No sir. I can tell by the way when he looks at you he only turns his head instead of his whole body. His drooping head just swings to one side. Did you have a good time?"  .

"Okay. Broke up kind of early though."

"What early? It's after one."

Mike looked at the kitchen curtains and wondered if they'd been washed since his mother had died. They were dingy white and sheer and made him think of nurses' stockings.

He took the lizard out of his pocket and stood it up on his open palm under the table.

"I'm going out tomorrow and buy myself a pair of shoes," his father said. "All my heels are worn down. I think that's what's making my back hurt. I read about it. You want to come and get yourself a pair?"

"No thanks, Dad. I don't need shoes."

Mike pressed his thumbnail into the seam that ran along the lizard's belly, remembering the plastic thread.

"I was glad to see you get out tonight. It's no good, you spending so much time in that room."

Mike balanced the lizard on his knee, then looked up and saw Chester standing in the doorway.

"Hey, com'ere Chester, you old shit," Mike said. "What do you think, huh? What do you think?" He ran his hands over the dog's face and down into the fur between its front legs. The lizard dropped from his knee to the floor. He scratched Chester's back and wrapped one hand around his tail. "I think we have to call you Old Chester. Old Chesterfield."

"You going out with her again?"

"Nah. She's too young."

Chester slipped under the table, lizard in mouth.

"At least you got out."

# BREAKFAST, LUNCH, AND DINNER

Food was there at the start. We met when he asked me to pass him a basket of cheddar cheese Goldfish. I was happy to do it because before he'd sat down I'd had those fish all to myself and had fallen into a rhythm of taking a sip, eating a fish, taking a sip, etc. I didn't want to give them up altogether, though, so I slid the basket along the bar until it was equidistant between us. He took a handful and said he hadn't had any dinner. I smiled and nodded as if to say I know what that's like, even though I didn't and don't. He put a couple of fish in his mouth, then shook the ones left in his fist like they were dice he was getting ready to throw.

After more nods and smiles from me and more fish rattling from him, he turned to get the bartender's attention. I selected a fish from the basket. Before I was able to put it in my mouth, he asked if he could buy me a drink. I said yes, using the hand that held the fish between thumb and index finger to gesture. I don't remember why a simple yes needed gestures—I was either thanking him excessively or taking a roundabout route to yes by way of no. I didn't put that fish in my mouth until he turned to pay for the drinks.

Our conversation moved by fits and starts through the better part of an hour. When I got up to leave he asked if I would meet him there the following night. I said I would and did. That second night, as it came to be known, we stayed until closing time then went to a diner where he ordered sausage and eggs, so I did too. He had his eggs up. I had mine scrambled. I didn't think I could handle all of that gooey yolk attractively.

He drove me back to my car and we kissed for a good long time in the parking lot. It was winter and there was a lot of wool coat between us. Driving home, I sat up straight and wished there were more cars on the road. I felt alert and outgoing. Driving, especially on the deserted road, didn't seem like enough to be doing.

He called me early the next morning and said he was tired but happy and asked me to dinner. In the restaurant, rubbing my knuckles with his thumbs, he said, "I don't want to scare you, but I think I'm falling in love." I said I thought I was too. That's when I started to cook.

I was unemployed so my days were spent getting ready. Like a European, I'd go to a butcher for meat, a fishstore for seafood, a vegetable market for produce, a bakery for bread, and—very important, we were new and nervous—to a liquor store for wine. I'd get back to my apartment around noon, deposit the various paper bags on the counter, then stand in front of the refrigerator and eat a half a tomato as if it was a cupcake, biting around the edges then popping the center in my mouth whole. I was too giddy to want to eat, and too concerned with how my stomach would look later in bed, but I didn't want hunger pangs interfering with my ability to concentrate on my cooking.

The recipes I was going to use had, of course, already been selected from the fat *Joy of Cooking*. I'd read through them to determine what needed to be done first. Veal might have to be submerged in marinade or chicken rinsed in cool water and set, uncovered, on a plate in the refrigerator. If I was making Caesar salad—he loved it and would eat even the soggiest leaves—olive oil (*none other,* the book warned) had to be poured into a glass jar with a clove of garlic. The jar had to be covered and set in the sun on the kitchen window sill. Several times during an afternoon, I'd pick up that jar, turn it over in my hands, and watch the garlic move through the oil.

I'd do everything I could except set the table—there is something sad about a table set for dinner at one-thirty in the afternoon—then go and take a long shower. I'd rinse determinedly until the hot water gave out because I'd read enough women's magazines to know the importance of rinsing. (Vidal Sassoon thinks you should rinse your hair until your arms ache. I think I was about ten when I read that interview.) When the water was colder than I could stand, I'd step out, wrap my head in a towel, then rub the bargain body lotion I was buying to counterbalance the expensive groceries, into my skin. Still moist in creases, I'd dress carefully but casually—I didn't want to look *dressed*—then it was back to the kitchen to turn the oil-and-garlic jar and wait until I could start cooking.

By the time I'd hear his car, everything would be just on the verge of readiness. I'd go and stand at the top of the stairs. As he'd make his way up we'd smile at one another, a little embarrassed but also genuinely relieved to be together again, as though each of us was afraid that the other had had a change of heart during the course of the day and decided to call the whole thing off.

As he'd pull me close I'd be aware of things bubbling and needing basting behind me. He'd sit down at the table. I'd show off at the stove. The final stages were flashy. I knew I looked like an expert, doing several things at once, all of them aromatic.

He'd pause after nearly every mouthful to tell me things were delicious. He'd have seconds, sometimes thirds. I'd been intensely involved with that food all day—inspecting, selecting, paying, washing, tossing, sautéing, serving—and was tired of it. With him there, handsome and husband-like in front of me, it couldn't get my attention. Anyway, not eating meant more prominent hipbones for later.

As the weeks passed it got easier to be with him. We moved through our meals with just the sounds of forks against plates and wine into glasses. Touching him, a finger on his forearm, a foot on his chair, seemed to complete the sensation of good food in my mouth.

No longer cooking with win-or-lose urgency, I was less familiar with the food by the time it made the table. I ate as much as he did. My stomach wasn't a factor any longer. However it was would be fine.

We went to restaurants a couple of times a week and ordered with complete abandon. We had appetizers, bottles of wine, and when the dinner plates were cleared, we had Grand Marnier with our coffee. There was an unspoken financial agreement: I bought the fixings for elaborate dinners and he picked up eighty-five-dollar checks.

We took the security we'd found at the table with us when we got up. After lunch one Saturday, we went shopping for a pair of shoes together. Looking in the store window, I leaned back and felt his belly in the small of my back. In a fit of contentment, he bought a pair of black shoes he was never going to put on without first saying he didn't know why he'd bought them. I'd see him reach for them and wait for him to say what he always said, "I hate these shoes."

Gradually I stopped using serving dishes. Food went from the pan to the plates. With an eye on my grocery bill, I cut out the wine. We drank iced tea or water. I no longer needed recipes. I knew about how long it took to cook a chicken or a chop and was confident enough to experiment with seasonings.

I began having to send him to the store for things I'd forgotten. He spent twenty minutes walking up and down supermarket aisles looking for capers. "Are they fish or vegetables or what?" he snapped when he got back.

By then he'd all but officially moved in. One morning we were up and getting dressed, not realizing the severity of the snowstorm outside, when his boss called and told him not to bother coming in, the roads were a mess. My mother was next. "You're not even thinking about driving are you?" I waited for my boss to call—I'd gotten a job answering the telephone in a a doctor's office—but he didn't. I left a message on his answering machine.

We got undressed and took our coffee back to bed with us. We thought we'd spend the whole day there, but in an hour we were up and hungry. We put on all the snow clothes we could find and walked the six blocks to the A & P. We bought eggs, cheese, English muffins, Canadian bacon, and a coffee cake. On the way home we passed one of those square trucks that deliver potato chips to people's houses. It was stuck in a driveway. He wanted to ask the driver if we could buy a tin of chips. "No," I said. "Come on. We have enough."

He spread a blanket on the living room floor while I went

to work in the kitchen. We turned on HBO, ate, snoozed, fooled around, and watched movies all day and into the night. At three o'clock in the morning we were wide awake watching a movie about a couple who did nothing but go for walks and talk. These two walked through endless parks and down city streets. They walked alongside rivers that blurred and became crowded outdoor markets. Most of their conversations were about dreams one or the other had had, long dreams that sounded like they were being made up on the spot. When I found myself waiting for the "and thens"—"And then, suddenly I was in hell . . . and then a girl I secretly loved in high school was there . . . and then I knew they were going to bury me alive"—I got up and turned it off. We crawled into bed to sleep some more.

When the alarm went off the next morning, I was already in the shower. He opened the bathroom door and asked me to please hurry up. I stayed in longer than I would have if he hadn't emphasized the please, then went into the kitchen to make coffee.

There were dishes in the sink and on the counters. The spatula was face down in the frying pan, bits of cheese on its edges. The milk had been left out and smelled sour, which put an end to the coffee since neither of us would drink it black.

In the living room, the blanket was still on the floor and the television was not in its usual spot. I didn't touch anything, didn't even throw out the sour milk.

When I went back into the bedroom, he was pulling on his pants. As I buttoned my skirt, I had the sense that we were competing to see which of us could get out into the white responsible world first.

He stopped volunteering to go to the supermarket without me. The tomatoes he'd brought back were always too soft, the pork chops too thick, anyway. We started food shopping together. My spirits would lift as we'd pull into the parking lot. I'd get to buy things I wouldn't have if he wasn't there to pay the bill. Like artichokes. Yogurt-covered peanuts. Spring water. He'd push the cart and I'd dart off and back again. When it took me a while to decide on something, he'd catch up to me. I'd know he was behind me because he'd tap me softly on the rear end with the cart.

Since he was paying for the groceries, dinners out became something I had to press to get. I knew as I opened a menu, large and leatherette, how to make trouble if I wanted to.

Towards the end of one scratchy Saturday afternoon, I gave him an ultimatum. "I want to go out," I said. We went to a gaudy twenty-fifth-anniversary kind of place where I, pushing hard, had ordered a second bottle of wine by the time a white-haired lady came to the table and asked if we'd like to have our picture taken. When he said no I said yes. She took it, six dollars was added to our bill, and he was furious.

I found his tight-fistedness so unattractive. The financial finagling that I was doing, the transfer of the grocery bill from me to him that I'd engineered, seemed somehow feminine and so my birthright.

A week later I got the picture in the mail. Our faces look fleshy and fixed, his in anger, mine in drunken I-dare-you.

We began to take food with us in the car. Like an alcoholic husband and wife with their mayonnaise jar of gin, we had our hard pretzels and Kit Kat bars.

We were getting ready to drive to the shore for the day—

the shore meant sausage and peppers, clams on the half shell. He was sitting out in the car waiting for me. I was on my way out the door when I realized we had no food for the way down. Nothing. I was in the kitchen putting pears in a plastic bag when I heard the car horn. I went to the window and looked out. He saw me and changed from one long blast to a series of short toots. I stood and listened. He leaned out of the car and shouted, "What's taking you?"

"Snacks," I shrieked back, stretching out the middle of the word so that it lasted for several seconds.


The end came when he had the courage to say out loud that all we shared was appetite. I knew he was right, had even tried to justify the situation to myself—other couples had the opera or the New York Mets—and failed. But there in the serious afternoon light, it was too humiliating to admit.

I tried to dislodge food from its spot at the top of our agenda. I checked the "What's Happening" column in Friday's paper. On Saturday morning I asked, "What do you want to do today?" as though we generally did things. I'd already chosen an antique auction, though neither one of us knew anything about old furniture beyond that we liked it in a vague sort of way.

He agreed to go immediately and said seventy miles wasn't too far to drive. There was a lot of chirpy conversation in the car. We commented on things as we passed them, deer and factory outlets.

After two sets of directions from pedestrians, we pulled up to a field that had rows of folding chairs on it. There were clusters of people in the first couple of rows only.

70

"Hasn't it started yet?" I asked one of two young men who were loading a bedroom set onto the back of a pick up.

"You kidding?" he said, slamming the gate of his truck closed. "It's in full swing."

The other guy seemed to understand how important the auction was to me and said, "Most of the dealers stayed away. The organizers are demanding a too-high percentage."

We stayed for a little while, sitting side-by-side in the otherwise empty fifth row.

On the way home we stopped and bought a pizza with extra cheese and mushrooms. I insisted on setting out plates and napkins before we opened the box.

We each had one piece pretty happily, but halfway through the second I was trying not to cry and having trouble swallowing. There seemed to be dry space in my mouth around the bite of pizza.

He looked at me then stood up. He tipped his plate over the garbage pail, put in in the sink, and said, "I'm going, okay? I'll call you." I nodded and kept nodding while I listened to him go down the stairs.

# WINTER RENTALS

There's an affair going on downstairs. He never spends the whole night. A couple of times a week I get woken up by the sound of his car starting. It's a big old thing, the bomb a family will keep around and make the father drive. The engine turns over on the third try. I lie in bed rooting for it. Then, most of the time, comes the high-pitched Japanese rev of her car. When tires have stopped crunching on gravel, I know it's safe to go back to sleep.

I think about them making the decision to rent the apartment. I love logistics. (I heard a story about an estranged wife who hired a helicopter to scatter leaflets containing damning personal information about her husband over a professional conference he was attending. Rather than having been there when the paper came down, although that wouldn't have been bad, I would have loved to be in the room when she set it up with the pilot.) About the apartment the man downstairs probably said, "Christ, we spend that much on hotel rooms every month." He looks like the kind of guy, square-jawed and skinny, who would begin a lot of his sentences with Christ. Then she said, "And we'll have a whole apartment with a beautiful view."

We all have views down here because we're in winter rentals, which means we've got beachfront apartments that go for big money during the summer. We're in in September, out in June.

I met Cathy at the laundromat. She's divorced and has an eight-year-old son. They live in one of these apartments every winter and camp out in a Pine Barren's campground every summer. She has high quality camping equipment and a year-round post office box. She knows a couple of other women, also divorced with kids, who do the same thing: winter rental, summer campground, p.o. box.

Cathy explained all of this time while we were folding sheets—she's the kind of person who always takes the sheet over when it's small enough for one person to handle. I can't help thinking that her situation sounds like a 60 Minutes segment. Poverty and the Single Parent. Morely Safer in a rumpled safari jacket pulling open the tent flap and looking inside. The camera showing you what he sees in there. "And when it rains?" he'd ask, sitting cross-legged on a log.

I am here in my winter rental because I didn't get into graduate school. I was sure I would get in so I didn't make an alternate life plan, unless you count some half-hearted motions I made toward moving in with a man who didn't want me living with him. On the way to look at a house—he's had it renting and has money in the bank—he threw a spectacular temper tantrum that included a U-turn against traffic. So much for house-hunting.

When the rejection letters came—they were thin, I knew

before I opened them—I had to make all of these bad phone calls to tell people. I'd get through the first part okay and then they'd say something and it would be my turn to talk again but I'd be crying so I couldn't. The silence would go on too long. I'd exhale or clear my throat so they'd know we hadn't been disconnected.

I took a proofreading job and hated it all summer. I got out of bed at four-thirty on a Saturday morning, made coffee, and sat down to some anxiety about the future. Since the prospect of graduate school had geared me up for a move, I wanted to make one. I'd heard about cheap rents at the Jersey shore so I got in my car, drove down here, went into a diner, and ate a cheese omelet very slowly while I looked at the winter rental listings. By nine-thirty I'd signed a lease. I'm here trying to write a novel and watching the couple downstairs.

I have an idea of how they met. Walking up the stairs to my apartment, I can't help looking directly into their kitchen window. On the table there are stacks and stacks of pamphlets and envelopes. There's apparently some sort of mass mailing going on. They must share an endangered species or a congressional candidate, which is probably what his wife thinks is taking up so much of his time.

The girl isn't married, I know because she sometimes spends the whole night. She's in her early twenties, big and athletic-looking, not at all the kind of person you'd expect to be involved in so well established an affair. I think she's a nurse, but I'm not sure why I think that. I must have seen her in a nurse's uniform at some point, but not lately.

Cathy resents them. To her, I guess, they're two people with three places to live, two permanent and one temporary. And here she is with just the temporary and the tent. Or maybe

75

there was another woman involved in the breakup of her marriage and her contempt for their affair is wifely. She always asks me about them, though, and when she comes over she goes right to the window to check for their cars.

We share a mailbox, me and the affair. They get once-a-month utility bills and that's it. One of them is T. Stanki. I figure it's her and her name is Theresa because every Theresa I've ever known has taken care of business.

Once or twice a week, Theresa (I need to call her something) will pull up in the middle of the day, carry a bag of groceries into the house, then come right back out and leave. Food shopping for an affair. You know she's got wine in that bag and three different kinds of cheeses.

In trashy novels, new couples always head into the kitchen right after the first time they have sex. Even though there is supposedly nothing to eat in the house, they find a half a bottle of wine, a nice hunk of cheese, some rice crackers, maybe a jar of olives. The woman says something like, "We managed to scrounge up . . ." Come on. If I were to take somebody into my kitchen when I hadn't been to the supermarket in a while, we'd be lucky to find an egg. We'd share an egg, boiled.


Theresa pulled up last night, usual time, but he never arrived. She stayed all night. They may not need the place the whole nine months. I hope she got him to pay the rent in advance.

Maybe she planned to spend the night alone. I figure she either lives with her parents or has a couple of roommates. She probably took a long, hot shower, put on a flannel nightgown and sweatsocks, watched a TV movie, then slept alone in the double bed.

Cathy's son Ronnie watches television from the minute he gets home from school until she makes him go to bed. She says she lets him because he doesn't get any all summer.

I was sitting at her kitchen table the other day. Ronnie was in the den with the television. Cathy was blow-drying her hair in the bedroom. Her phone bill was right in front of me, the total-amount-due card on top. I looked. Three hundred and eleven dollars, previous balance zero.

I wonder if they know I watch them. They probably make cracks about me like the ones I used to make about an old woman who lived across the street from my last apartment. She watched all day, this old lady did, always in her robe. I pretended to resent her but actually found her interest kind of flattering. I worried that I wasn't fun to watch.

I liked her after I saw her call one of the neighborhood little girls over—the kid was the child of vegetarians, her dresses were hand-smocked—and show her how to make a diamond ring by catching a firefly and smearing it on her finger. "Wait until it gets dark, honey. Wait until dark."


Cathy and I make fun of our apartments. They're over-furnished for one thing, right down to too many magnets on the refrigerators. We point at nautical decorations and get hysterical. The owners of these places must think summer renters want a crash course in ocean.

When I first got here I thought I'd leave it all up, even the big plastic crabs that were nailed to the bathroom wall. But I couldn't do it. I filled two drawers right to the top with starfish and the heads of sea captains. I'm stuck with some of it. The shower curtain with shells and their Latin names on it. The lamp the base of which is a cresting wave. Cathy hasn't

77

touched anything in her place. She says she'd no more do that than she'd rearrange the pictures on the wall in a restaurant.


The library down here is sort of an anti-library. They don't have a card catalogue; you just look around. And they play music. A couple of days ago they had a tape of Christmas carols going. The librarian was singing along, loud. She has a good voice but no sense that a library is supposed to be quiet.

I think she thinks I'm an egghead because I take out serious stuff and return it quickly. It's amazing how long you can stay with a book—you're only half aware of the day going by—when the alternative to reading is walking from room to room. I made it through *Moby Dick*. Read and reread *Madame Bovary*. Finished all of the Dickens I could find. I have a Joyce and an Austen out now, two substantial figures who got by me altogether in college.

I feel like a jerk when it seems like I'm trying to set up my own private graduate school. Like when you were eleven and didn't get invited to the birthday party of the kid in your class who had a built-in pool, so your parents went out and bought some shitty wading pool and told you, "Don't worry. We'll have our own swim party here." Things like that made you wonder how they ever got to be as old as they were.


I walk a lot down here. After spending the morning pacing around my typewriter drinking coffee, I need to get out. The last time I talked to my sister she asked me how and what I was doing. Writing, walking, watching the people downstairs, I told her. And can I borrow a hundred dollars? She said she can't walk alone on the beach. It makes her too self-con-

scious, like she's pondering the meaning of life out there. I know what she means. I feel too much like a writer agonizing over my work. I have more writerly thoughts in the supermarket when my face is cold and I can hear the voices of the checkers.

## ABOUT THE AUTHOR

**Agnes Rossi** lives in New Jersey. A graduate of Rutgers University, she is currently enrolled in the creative writing program at New York University. In 1985 she was the recipient of a grant for prose from the New Jersey State Council on the Arts. She is also the winner, along with the poet William Allen, of the 1986 publication prize of the Creative Writing Department of New York University. The judge was Susan Minot.